A modern approach

Reading and writing sh ... natural activities and inte ... ... the child. The next most important aid is a series of books designed to stimulate and interest him and to give daily practice at the right level.

Educational experts from five Caribbean countries have co-operated with the author to design and produce this Ladybird Sunstart Reading Scheme. Their work has been influenced by (a) the widely accepted piece of research 'Key Words to Literacy[1]' adapted here for tropical countries. This word list has been used to accelerate learning in the early stages. (b) The work of Dr. Dennis Craig[2] of the School of Education, U.W.I., and other specialists who have carried out research in areas where the English language is being taught to young children whose natural speech on entering school is a patois or dialect varying considerably from standard English.

[1] Key Words to Literacy by J McNally and W Murray,
    published by The Teacher Publishing Co Ltd,
    Derbyshire House, Kettering, Northants, England.

[2] An experiment in teaching English by Dennis R Craig,
    Caribbean Universities Press, also Torch (Vol. 22, No. 2),
    Journal of the Ministry of Education, Jamaica.

THE LADYBIRD SUNSTART READING SCHEME consists of six books and three workbooks. These are graded and written with a controlled vocabulary and plentiful repetition. They are fully illustrated.

Book 1 'Lucky dip' (for beginners) is followed by Book 2 'On the beach'. Workbook A is parallel to these and covers the vocabulary of both books. The workbook reinforces the words learned in the readers, teaches handwriting and introduces phonic training.

Book 3 'The kite' and Book 4 'Animals, birds and fish' follow Books 1 and 2, and are supported by Workbook B. This reinforces the vocabulary of Books 3 and 4 and again contains handwriting exercises and phonic training.

Book 5 'I wish' and Book 6 'Guess what?' with Workbook C complete the scheme.

The illustrated handbook (free) for parents and teachers is entitled 'A Guide to the Teaching of Reading'.

For classroom use there are two boxes of large flash cards which cover the first three books.

Published by Ladybird Books Ltd
80 Strand London WC2R 0RL
A Penguin Company
10 9 8 7 6 5 4

Printed in Italy

BOOK 2
The Ladybird SUNSTART Reading Scheme
(a 'Key Words' Reading Scheme)

On the beach

by W. MURRAY

with illustrations
by MARTIN AITCHISON

Ladybird Books Ltd
in collaboration with Longman Caribbean Ltd

a girl  a boy

Joy   Ken

You see a girl.
She is Joy.

You see a boy.
He is Ken.

Joy and Ken
look at a man.
He is a big man.

---

new words   Joy   Ken

Ken knows the man.
He likes him.

Joy knows him
and she likes him.

The man knows the girl
and the boy.

He likes Joy and Ken.

---

new words   knows   likes   him

read

write

Joy can read and write.

She likes to write
in the sand.

She wants to write to Ken.

Joy writes to Ken
in the sand.

She says to him,
Look at that, Ken.
Can you read that?

new words   read   write   sand

Ken, Look. I can write. Joy

Ken sees Joy
write in the sand.

He wants to write.

He writes in the sand
and says to Joy,
Look at this, Joy.
Read this.
Can you read this?

---

new word   this

Ken likes to play.
He wants to play
on the sand.

Come on, says Ken.
You come and play.
Please come and play.
This is for you.

---

new words   play   on

This is for you, says Joy.
This water is for you.

They play on the sand.
They play in the water.

The man they know
is in the water.
Ken and Joy see him.

---

new words   they   water

fish   boat

The man wants to fish.
He has a boat.
He is in the boat.
It is on the water.

Ken and Joy can see him
in the boat.
It is a little boat.

new words   fish   has   boat

Ken and Joy like to fish.
They look for fish
in the water.

Ken has one.
He has a little fish.

Come and look at this,
he says to Joy.
I have one.

---

new word   have

nets

men

You can see nets.
The nets are for the fish.
The men come for the nets.
They want to fish.

Ken and Joy look at
the men and the nets.

new words   nets   men   are

The boats are
on the water.

The men have the nets
in the boats.
Off they go.

The men go off
in the boats.
They go off to fish.

---

new words   off   go

The men go off to sea
in the boats.

They have the nets.

The nets go into the sea.
They go into the sea
for the fish.

The fish go into the nets.

new words   sea   into

The men are on the beach.

They have the nets.

They pull the nets.

They pull the nets in.

Fish are in the nets,
big fish and little fish.

---

new words   beach   pull

Ken and Joy
are with the men
on the beach.

They see the men
with some fish.
Pull, pull, they say.
Pull the nets in.

Some birds see the fish.

---

new words   some   with

women

Some women are on the beach.

They see the men with fish.
The women want some fish.

They come to buy some.
They buy some fish
on the beach.

---

new words   women   buy

children

ball

The children are in the sea
They like to play
in the water.

The children have a ball.
It is a big ball.

They see women
and children on the beach.

new words   children   ball

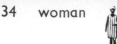
Mummy   Daddy

I want the ball, says Ken.

You can have it, says Joy.

The children can see that
a man and a woman
are on the beach.

I see Mummy and Daddy,
says Joy.

new words   woman   Mummy   Daddy

bag

Yes, says Ken.
I see Mummy and Daddy.

The two children go to
Mummy and Daddy.

Joy sees that Mummy
has a bag.

Ken sees that Daddy
has a box.

---

new words   Yes yes bag

Can we eat, please,
says Ken.

Yes, we want to eat,
says Joy.

We all want to eat,
says Daddy.

Mummy and Daddy
and the two children
all eat on the beach.

---

new words   we   eat   all

Joy looks to see
what she can find
on the beach.

She looks on the sand.
She looks in the sea.

She has a bag.

Mummy is with Joy.
She looks to see what
she can find for Joy.

---

new words   what   find

Joy says to Ken,
Come and see
what you can find.

No, says Ken.
No, thank you.
I want to play with Daddy.

Ken has his ball.
He plays with his Daddy.

---

new words   No   no   his

The ball goes up.
It goes into a tree.

Ken goes up the tree
for the ball.
He likes to go up the tree.

Daddy looks up at him.

new words   goes   up

an orange

Look at me, Joy, says Ken
Look at me, up this tree.
You come up the tree.

No, says Joy.
No, thank you.
I want an orange.

She sees that Mummy
has an orange.

---

new words   me   an   orange

Mummy has an orange
for Joy.
One for you, Joy, she says.

I want an orange,
says Ken.
One for me, please.

Yes, one for you,
says Mummy.
One for you, Ken.

---

no new words

Read the words with the help of the pictures.
Then cover the pictures and read the words.

1   Ken plays with sand and water.

2   Some oranges are in this bag. She eats
    an orange. We all like oranges.

3   Has he a ball? No, he has a fish.

4   Off you go, she says to the bird.

5   The boy is on a box. Pull me up, he says.

6   Have you a bag, the woman says.
    Yes, says Mummy.

7   Daddy buys a ball for Ken.

8   He goes up the tree for his ball.

9   Joy looks on the beach to see
    what she can find.

10 The women know the men. They see
    the men go into the sea for the nets.

11 He reads and she writes.

12 The children see him go in the boat.

All the 49 new words in this book are on
this page.

Words new to the series used in this book

Cover: on beach *(see below)*

Total number of words 49